NOT EVEN THEN

IT WAS ENOUGH

NISWITA SINGH

Made with ♥ on the Notion Press Platform
www.notionpress.com

Not Even Then

by

Niswita Singh

Contents

Foreword vii

Preface ix

Acknowledgements xi

Prologue xiii

LETTERS

1. BALCONY   3

2. SHADOW   5

3. THREAD   8

4. HUNGER   10

5. BONE   12

6. MIRROR   14

7. DUST   17

8. STATIC   19

9. HOLLOW   22

10. STILL   25

ECHOES

11. TINDER   31

12. PHANTOM   34

13. MOLT   38

14. CELLER   41

15. CRADLE   44

16. SCAB   47

17. KNELL   50

18. RELIQUARY   53

Contents

19. THRESHOLD   56

20. NOT EVEN THEN   59

Author's Note   63

About the Author   65

Foreword

I didn't write this book because I wanted to. I wrote it because I had to.

There are things we carry that no one sees. Bruises shaped like silence. Memories we never consented to. Rooms inside us where the lights flicker and no one ever knocks. This book is made of such rooms. It is stitched together with late-night thoughts, the kind that arrive when the world is quiet and grief grows teeth.

Not Even Then is not a story, really. It's a conversation. A confession. A reaching out. Each chapter, each letter, is a kind of unraveling—of one girl speaking to her younger self, trying to remember, trying to forget, and failing at both.

I don't expect this book to fix anything. But maybe, just maybe, it can sit beside someone in their own dark room and whisper, you are not alone.

If you've ever been haunted by a memory, woken up at 3 a.m. and felt like a ghost in your own skin, or looked in the mirror and not recognized who's looking back—this book is for you.

And if none of this makes sense now, maybe it will one day.

Or maybe not even then.

—Niswita

Preface

This book was born quietly.

Not in a moment of inspiration, but in many moments of breaking. It came together between long pauses, between unanswered texts, between the hush of grief and the hum of memory. It wasn't meant to be a book at first. Just fragments—letters, thoughts, sentences I wrote when I couldn't sleep. But over time, those fragments began to form a voice. And that voice sounded like someone I used to be.

Not Even Then is not linear. It doesn't move from beginning to end. It spirals. It returns. It forgets and remembers. It grieves and still hopes. It is about a girl who writes without knowing she's already gone, and about another girl who reads and begins to understand why everything hurt so much.

This book does not aim to teach, redeem, or justify. It only wants to feel. To be real. To exist the way pain does—unapologetically and without reason.

If it finds you at the right time, I hope it holds your hand.

And if not—perhaps you'll come back to it, someday.

Not for answers.

But for honesty.

Acknowledgements

To every trembling hand that's ever held a pen and still chose to write — I see you. Thank you.

This book would not exist without the quiet strength of every person who shared a story, who stayed up late listening, who held space for my silences, or gently reminded me that pain doesn't make us unlovable.

To my readers: thank you for letting Diya and Zill sit beside you, even when their truths felt too heavy to hold. Thank you for reading between the hurt, for feeling what I could barely say.

To the people who believed in this story before I did — you gave it breath.
To the ones who stayed — you gave it heart.
And to the ones I lost — you gave it reason.

A soft, infinite thank you to the shadows that didn't stay shadows forever.

And to the girl I used to be: you made it. You wrote it. You're still here.

With all my love,
— Niswita

Prologue

There was a red anklet once.

It was small, barely a thread, almost nothing. But I swear—I swear—it held a scream in every knot. A story in every loop. I wore it before I even knew what it meant. Before I knew what leaving felt like. Before I knew that you could still disappear even when your body remains.

No one remembers the first time they vanish. It doesn't happen all at once. It happens in soft, forgettable ways. A skipped meal. A name no longer called. The sound of laughter you used to recognize, now foreign. It happens slowly—like dusk pretending not to be night.

This is not a love story. Not in the way you think. It is a remembering. A reckoning. A girl, writing from a place you cannot find on any map, to another girl who still believes the world can be forgiven.

If you are reading this, you are part of it now.

And I'm sorry.

But some truths only survive when whispered between the lines.

Some ghosts only speak when no one is listening.

LETTERS

For the girl I couldn't save

and the one who still lives in me.

1

BALCONY

"The saddest part of drowning is not the water — it's knowing no one will come looking."

October 8, 2024

You ran like no one told you the ground could betray you. Like joy was still an option. Barefoot, wild hair, two missing teeth, red thread tangled around your ankle like it was trying to hold you still.

You don't know I watch you. Every evening, same hour. From the rusted balcony where I keep forgetting I can't plant new things anymore.

Your laugh is too loud. Too full. The kind that makes people turn around before they smile. I used to laugh like that. Before the world told me there was nothing funny about girls like me.

The dog follows you like he remembers someone else in your footsteps. Maybe he does. I fed him when he was a puppy. He never barked when I cried. That's loyalty. Or something closer to recognition.

Today I wanted to call out. Say your name—if I knew it. Warn you, maybe. Or ask you to look up and see me.

But I didn't. The words got stuck in my throat like they've been stitched shut.

There's a silence that comes after survival. It's not peace. It's more like an echo that never quite stops. And I'm full of it. Heavy with what I never said in time.

You don't know me. But I know you.

You are what I must have looked like before they decided I was too much.
Before he said, "You wanted it."
Before they asked me, "But why were you even there?"

I didn't plan to write this. But my hands have been itching for days. And the ink smells like something I haven't touched in a long time.

If you ever hear your name said like it's a warning, run. And if you ever feel your joy slipping—grab it by the throat. Don't let it leave you behind like mine did.

I'm writing this from somewhere between sky and soil. Close enough to remember.
Far enough that I don't know if I'm still real.

But I saw you.
And that felt like something.

2
SHADOW

———❦———

"Some things rot quietly — not out of decay, but out of silence too long swallowed."

October 10, 2024

You were crying today.

Not loud. Not for attention. That small, quiet kind of crying that kids aren't supposed to know how to do yet. But I saw it. I saw you kick the dirt in that alley beside the yellow gate. Your back was to the world, and your fists were in your sleeves.

I wanted to scream. Or climb down. Or punch something for you.

Instead, I watched.

Like a coward.

Like I did when it happened to me.

You remind me of the version of myself I buried when I was still learning how to pronounce "no" with a voice that didn't shake.

You're my shadow. I've known that since the second time I saw you, right down to the chipped nail polish and the left sock always falling off. You carry pieces of me like you don't even know they're broken.

And the red anklet?

I almost threw up when I saw it.

Mine is still here. Somewhere in this room. Still red. Still whole.

He gave it to me. Wrapped it around my ankle like a promise.

Then made it into something I couldn't scrub off.

"She's too friendly."

"She laughs with boys."

"She's not the type to be believed."

I kept that anklet on even after. I thought it would change if I did. But it didn't. It just got tighter. Started whispering things to me.

By the end, it was the only thing left around my body.

When you ran by today, I noticed it again—loose on your ankle, free. You don't know what it can become yet. That's why I'm writing. Because someone should've warned me before it was too late.

And maybe it's already too late for you too.

I hope not.

God, I hope not.

But if it is—

I'll still be here. Writing. Watching. Wanting you to look up.

If someone tells you to be quiet when you're in pain—don't.

If they ask for proof of what your body remembers—walk away.

And if they don't believe you, not even when you shatter in front of them—

Then know:
You're not alone.

3

THREAD

"My hands shake not from fear, but from holding on too long to things that never held me back."

October 13, 2024

The sky smelled like burnt sugar tonight. That kind of air that makes you think of childhood and ash at the same time.

I saw you trip over the curb, laugh, then pretend you meant to fall. That kind of grace only belongs to children and ghosts.

The thread was still there—red and stubborn. You dragged it through a rain puddle and didn't care it soaked the hem of your trousers. I hated how much that did to me. The rage of it. The tenderness of it. I almost bit my lip until it bled.

He tied that thread around my ankle the night he said he loved me. And I—god—believed him. Not because I was stupid. But because I wanted to be believed too. About anything.

No one ever tells you that being believed is a form of survival.

When I told the truth—his truth—my voice cracked. Not from fear. From disbelief at how easily it was thrown back at me. They said I smiled too much. Had too many male friends.

That I must've misread the night. The thread stayed on, long after he left. A noose in disguise.

And one morning, I looked down and it wasn't wrapped around my ankle anymore.
It was around my neck.

I keep wondering if this is why I see you. If somehow the thread pulled me here—to witness, to scream without sound, to beg silently across a balcony you never look up to.

Do you feel it tightening yet?
Or are you still in the part where it feels like love?

If it ever starts to choke—
don't wait to be believed.
Cut it off.

Burn it if you have to.

4

HUNGER

"Mothers leave in more ways than one. Some simply forget the sound of your name."

October 16, 2024

The dog didn't come today.

You came alone. You looked behind you more than once, but not up. Never up.

There's a hunger inside me now. Not for food—I stopped feeling that kind of hunger long ago. But for proof. That I'm still here. That I matter. That the air shifts when I move.

The hunger is cruel. It eats memory first.

I tried to make tea this morning. Walked into the kitchen, opened the cabinet, reached for the tea leaves—and my hand passed through the tin.

I dropped to the floor. I stayed there a long time. Watching dust float like it had more right to be alive than me.

I'm sorry. I didn't mean to say that out loud.
But maybe I did.

You remind me of the girl I was before the world tore holes in her. The girl who wanted to be a painter.

The girl who made songs out of spoon clinks and wind.

I stopped singing the day my boyfriend said, "Stop acting dramatic."

It was after the second time.

After I said no, again, and he laughed and said, "You said yes the first time, what's the difference?"

The difference was me.

But I lost me somewhere between no and never again.

Now, I watch you chase your shadow down the alley. I see you spinning, dizzy, oblivious to the darkness that lives in doorways. I want to grab your wrists and say, Don't go where I went. But I don't think my hands work like that anymore.

The hunger doesn't fade. It deepens.

I wonder if that's what grief really is—just hunger for a version of you no one remembers.

I don't want you to be remembered like I was.

As someone who was once bright.

As someone who was once believed to be fine.

I want you to stay.

Not for me.

But for yourself.

Please—stay.

5
BONE

"Every girl learns eventually: softness is dangerous, especially when it grows teeth."

October 18, 2024

Today the wind carried the scent of wet earth and burnt something. Like a funeral passed by too quickly.

You sat under the neem tree, cradling the stray's head in your lap like he was born from your skin. He looked at you the way he used to look at me—like he knew the weight I carried in my spine. Like he wanted to carry it too.

But he wouldn't come near the balcony.
Wouldn't even glance in my direction.
That's new.

I tried calling out—not with words. Just with want. It didn't work.

You fed him a piece of roti, broke it like communion. He licked your palm, and I swear my chest cracked. There's no other word for it. It cracked open like bone too close to the edge of skin.

He was my only friend in the end. And he stayed quiet, even as the voices in my head grew louder than thunder in tin roofs. I once told him everything. In whispers. In sobs.

He never judged me for not fighting harder. Or for coming undone.

You touched his ear the way I used to. You called him "Laaloo."
My name. The name I gave him.
How do you know?
I want to ask, but I can't. My throat is dry with old dust and unsaid truths.
Maybe this is hell. Maybe this is what it means to not rest: watching yourself be rewritten by someone else's innocence.
I dreamt last night. I was back in my room —the one with the cracked mirror and the posters I was too old for. But I couldn't touch anything. My fingers passed through the bed. The walls didn't hold sound. And the red anklet swung from the ceiling fan.
I didn't want to look up. But I did.
And I saw myself.
Barefoot. Swinging. Silent.
My bones still remembering the weight of being disbelieved.
I think I died in that room.
But the calendar still says October.
The dog still remembers my name.
And you—you still wear the anklet like it's just an ornament.
God, I hope it stays that way.
I want to believe it won't end for you the way it did for me.
But some things are passed down like blood.
Like bone.

6

MIRROR

"No one ever teaches you how to grieve someone who is still breathing."

October 22, 2024

There are no reflections here.

Not in the window. Not in the doorknob.

Not even in the broken shard I've kept tucked in the drawer for years.

I should have noticed earlier. But I didn't.

I kept wiping the mirror, thinking it was fogged.

You left chalk drawings on the road today. A girl with long hair, and a dog beside her. You wrote a name under it in curly letters—"Diya"—then quickly rubbed it out before anyone saw.

Why?

You don't know me.

You shouldn't know me.

I watched you from the balcony, shaking. It wasn't cold, but my hands couldn't stop trembling. Something inside me shouted—but it was like yelling underwater.

Do you hear me?

Do you feel me?

Or am I just folding into your dreams the way ghosts fold into silence?

You don't look scared. Not yet. But you glance around more now. You squint toward my building like a memory's trying to surface. You always look away before you reach the third floor. And I don't know if it's because you can't see me—or because you can.

When I was nine, I stood in front of the mirror and told myself: I will not be soft anymore. I will not be sweet. I will not be a girl who gets left behind.
I said it over and over until my mouth bled from the pressure.

And still, I was left.
By friends. By family. By a world that didn't believe me unless I wore bruises like badges.

I screamed when I saw myself in the mirror after that night.
I didn't recognize my face.
It looked like I'd swallowed every word I never said—and they were clawing to get out.

You must never feel this way. You must never look in a mirror and see someone else's violence in your own eyes.

So promise me:
If they touch you and laugh—don't laugh back.

If they blame your walk, your voice, your clothes, your freedom—don't change.
If they love you with closed fists and smiling lies—don't stay.

And if they ever make you question your memory—write it down.
Carve it somewhere they can't reach.
Let the truth become a home inside your chest.
Because once the mirror forgets you—
It's too late to remember yourself.

7
DUST

"There are ghosts louder than screams — they hum lullabies in your bones."

October 26, 2024

The neighbors were burning old clothes today. A pile of fabric catching fire like it had been waiting for years. Some pieces refused to burn—synthetic, stubborn. They just curled at the edges, blackened, and gave up smoke instead.

I wonder if that's what I did.

Burned just enough to be unrecognizable.

Not enough to disappear.

You walked by in a new dress. Green with little white birds on it. You twirled once, tripped over a stone, and kept twirling like the earth owed you rhythm. And for a moment, I could almost pretend everything was okay. That it never happened. That I never happened.

But then the dog came behind you, tail down, head low—and stopped right in front of the stairs. Just stopped. Stared. Not at you.

At me.

And he whimpered.

That sound—low, knowing—split something inside me.

I hadn't heard my name in days.

I don't know if it still belongs to me.

I opened the door to go down. But the lock... it wasn't locked. It wasn't even there. Just a door that didn't need unlocking. I touched the knob. My hand passed through.

And that's when it hit me.

I haven't left this house in weeks.

Not since the rope.

Not since the fan.

Not since the silence.

No one came to knock.

No one came to find me.

You came close today. You looked at the building, then at the windows, then straight through the space where I stood. Your eyes didn't flinch. Didn't pause. They just... moved on.

That's how the world forgets us.

Not with cruelty.

With indifference.

"If a girl disappears but no one asks why, did she ever exist at all?"I don't know what's worse—dying, or watching someone else live the life you could have had.

But I'm still here.

Covered in dust.

Waiting for you to see what no one else would.

"Love didn't abandon me. It just never knocked."

Chapter 8: Static

October 30, 2024

There's a radio in the living room that won't stop humming. It doesn't play music. Just static. Always static. Like it's trying to speak in a language only the dead can understand.

I pressed every button. Unplugged it. Nothing.

Maybe that's what I've become—static. Not a voice. Not a person. Just noise behind the sound of other people's lives.

You dropped something today.

A red anklet.

It slipped off your foot while you were running, landed in the middle of the road, and you didn't even notice. I nearly screamed. Not because it's yours—but because it's mine. The same one. The thread unraveled just enough for me to see the beads I strung myself. The way the charm leans slightly to the left. The way the color has faded from rage to rot.

I don't know how it got to you.
I don't want to know.
I used to believe objects can't carry memories.
But this one carries everything.

My shame. My silence. The last breath I took while begging to be believed.
You picked it up, looked around—and then you looked up.
Directly at me.
No hesitation.
No blinking.
Just... knowing.
And I swear, for a split second—
you saw me.
Not like a stranger.
Not like a shadow.
But like someone you'd already met.
Like someone you missed.
Like someone who still mattered.
I couldn't breathe. I still can't.
You tied the anklet to your schoolbag and walked away, dragging my memory with you. Not out of cruelty. Out of unknowing.
Maybe this is how grief survives: in things we think are ours, but belong to those who didn't get a second chance.

If you ever feel a weight on your back for no reason—
It's not guilt.
It's me.
Not to scare you.
Not to haunt you.
Just to say: I'm still here.

And I never wanted to be.

9
HOLLOW

—♡—

"Some letters are too heavy to send. So we bury them inside ourselves."

November 2, 2024

The lights flickered again tonight.

Not in a power-outage way. Not in a "someone call the electrician" way. But in a someone doesn't belong here anymore way.

You were drawing again—this time on paper. You used crayons, pressing so hard the red broke. It snapped, and you didn't flinch. Just kept going with the smaller piece like it was enough.

I watched from the usual place. Third floor. Left window. My hands against the pane, though I know it won't fog from breath anymore.

You looked up.
I froze.
But you looked through me again. Or past me. Or... into me?
Your eyes didn't carry fear.
But you looked sad. The kind of sadness that doesn't belong

22

to a child. Like someone else's grief was sitting inside your ribcage.

You had written my name in the corner of the page. Diya. Curved and careful.

Then you scratched it out so violently I thought the paper would tear.

I can't remember the last time I said my own name out loud.

My voice doesn't echo here.

It vanishes before it leaves my mouth.

Like this whole place is a vacuum sucking back every word I ever meant to say.

The mirror in my room shattered today. Not cracked—shattered. But I didn't hear it. I only noticed when I saw shards spread across the floor like teeth.

I stepped through them barefoot. Nothing cut. Nothing bled.

I think I know now.

I think I've known.

The rope.

The fan.

The silence.

I remember the last text I sent.

"Please believe me."

No one replied.

But they saw it.

Left it on read.

I think I stayed because I was unfinished. Because no one came. Because I didn't want to be forgotten like every other girl who said, "It wasn't my fault," and got buried anyway.

You wear my anklet like it means something. Like it still holds story.

I don't know if I want you to keep it.
Or throw it into fire.
   Do you feel me?
   Am I your shadow?
Or are you mine?

10

STILL

"I didn't want to be remembered. I just wanted to be found before I disappeared."

November 7, 2024

I felt it before I saw you.

Something in the air cracked. The silence wasn't silence anymore—it was a scream held too long in a small mouth.

You walked slower today. Head down. Anklet gone.

Your dress was buttoned wrong. Your lips bitten raw. There was dirt on your palms, like you'd been clawing at the earth or yourself.

And I knew.

Before you said anything.

I knew.

Zill, I swear, I tried.

I watched. I warned. I wrote.

I stayed.

But I couldn't stop him.

The man with the good smile. The neighbor with the soft laugh. The one who always brought sweets and patted your head too long.

I saw you flinch when he passed last week. I saw how you avoided his eyes, how your dog growled low in his throat, how you tucked your knees tighter when he was near.

I should have known it would happen.
I did know.

But I believed—
God, I believed—
that maybe this time, the world would spare you.
That maybe my haunting was enough.
That maybe I mattered in some invisible way.

And now you carry it.
The thing I died with.

Inside your body.
Inside your silence.

You came to the neem tree again. No anklet. No dog.
You didn't look up this time.
You looked inward.

And then you whispered,
"I didn't want it."
That's all. Just that.

And every window in this building shattered.

I knelt at the edge of the balcony, pressed my fists against my mouth, and I sobbed. No sound came out.
Because the dead don't get to scream.

You do.
And you must.
Zill—
don't let them tell you it's your fault.
Don't let them bury you in silence like they buried me.

If you ever find this letter, let it hold you. Let it prove that someone saw you—even if too late.

And if you wonder whether you'll be okay someday—

If you ask when it gets easier, when the guilt softens, when the hurt stops haunting your sleep—

I wish I could tell you yes.

I wish I could lie.

But the truth is—

not even then.

—Diya

ECHOES

For every girl who screamed without sound.

For every silence that should've been listened to.

For her.

For you.

11

TINDER

"I was not buried. I just stopped being remembered."*

I used to think silence was just the absence of sound.
Now I know it has a texture. It has a weight.
It clings like wet cloth, it seeps like water through floorboards, it breathes like something living.
And it follows me.
There is no page anymore.
No envelope, no name, no destination.
Just me, and the thing that keeps pulsing under my skin—
the thing I still, stupidly, call memory.
I don't know when it happened.
That moment I stopped writing to you.
Or stopped pretending you were someone other than myself.
Or stopped pretending I was still someone at all.
Sometimes I think I am a bruise stretched out over time.
Softening. Spreading.
But never quite fading.
I carry so many sounds that no one else can hear.
The river at dawn. My mother's anklets clicking on the floor.

The way my own name used to taste in someone else's mouth.

I remember light more than I remember time.
The way it struck the side of the house that day she left.
The shimmer on the water when I almost drowned,
and how, for a moment, I wanted to.
The ache is quieter now. That's how I know I'm not alive.
Pain, real pain, is noisy.
It howls. It kicks the walls.
This... this is different.
This is ache as atmosphere.
This is grief without grammar.
I do not walk anymore. I drift.
Sometimes I stand in the middle of an old room and forget where the walls are.
Sometimes I hear a girl laughing on the road and wonder if she's mine, or if I'm hers.
Sometimes I forget I ever had a body. And then the remembering hurts too much.
You see, when the dying is slow, the dead don't notice it.
We just keep speaking, hoping someone will look up.
We just keep loving, long after our names are forgotten.
The red thread is still around my ankle.
It burns colder now. It used to hum when I walked.
I don't walk anymore.

I know I'm supposed to say something important here.
Something final. Or wise.
But all I have is this dusk.
And the way it wraps around me like a mother who never

meant to stay.
    I am not writing anymore.
I am just
still.

12

PHANTOM

—♡—

"Some ghosts don't haunt houses. They haunt moments."

The noise began when the silence got too loud.

It started as a hum, almost tender—like the leftover sound in a room after the music ends. Then it grew teeth. It crackled. It whispered. It interrupted my memories mid-sentence. I try to remember my mother's voice and all I get is that static, slicing through her syllables like a dull knife. I try to remember the smell of the kitchen, and all I get is smoke. Nothing burns here, but everything smells like it already did.

This place I'm in—it isn't a room. It isn't a grave either. It's more like an echo chamber where the past folds in on itself and makes a shape out of me. Some mornings I wake up inside someone else's scream. Some nights I'm just a ripple on a wall.

I see flashes. Like old films being projected onto a broken sheet: —My father's slippers by the door.
—Zill tying her braid too tight.
—My wrist under the water, thin and pale like something already gone.
—A man calling my name like he owned it.

—A cupboard that swallowed the sound of my crying.

But none of it is stable. I reach for one image and another bleeds through. Grief here is not chronological. It is a glitch in the system. Every memory overlaps like poorly stacked glass—cutting me from angles I don't see coming.

Sometimes, I hear a radio playing. But only for a second. A line of a song. A half-spoken name. Then nothing.
It's like someone's trying to find me.
Or maybe I'm trying to find someone who never existed.

They say the dead are remembered by what they leave behind.
But what if all I left was confusion?
A handful of notebooks. A red thread. A girl who didn't understand her own sorrow.

There are voices, too.
But they don't speak words.

They just say you, you, you, like a warning.
Or a blame.

I scream sometimes, though I don't think it reaches anywhere.
The sound goes flat. Like screaming underwater.

It is cruel, isn't it?
That a body can rot in one place while the mind keeps wandering.
I was not brave enough to end it.
But I was not soft enough to keep going either.

And now I'm here. In between.
Half-noise. Half-shadow.
I think even the silence is forgetting me.

There was a time I thought pain was something that happened to you.

Now I understand—it's something that becomes you.

I don't know how long I've been like this.

I measure time by the flickers in my chest.

By the thoughts I can no longer hold.

I am not healing. I am just rearranging my wounds into new shapes.

Static. That's what I am now.

A transmission that never made it.

A signal swallowed by the void.

A girl trying to remember who she was before she became a noise no one tuned into.

37

13

MOLT

"Some rooms remember. Even after you forget."
There's a hallway in my mind I can't stop walking.
It's narrow. Peeling paint. A single bulb that flickers like it's afraid of the dark it's supposed to chase away.
And every door I pass leads to a room I've lived in.
A room that has lived in me.
The first door on the left opens to my childhood.
The cot with the uneven leg. The window that always stuck halfway.
There's a girl sitting cross-legged on the floor. She's drawing suns with black crayons.
Her shadow doesn't match her shape.
I close the door quickly.
Second one—my mother's bedroom.
It still smells like mustard oil and sharp things left unsaid.
Her sari is draped over the chair like it still remembers the shape of her back.
I look for her bangles on the bedside table.
They're gone.
But the sound remains.
That soft clinking—like distant rain on glass.

I don't go inside.

Third room—I can't even tell whose it was.
It's dim. The fan turns too slowly, like it's struggling to forget something.
There's a mirror on the wall, covered in a white cloth.
I have no memory of covering it.
But I know why I did.
They say mirrors are dangerous after death.
They hold the last image.
What if mine was not a face but a scream?
Further down the hall—my teenage room.
The only place I ever tried to become something.
The ceiling still has the constellation stickers I glued on the night my first friend stopped speaking to me.
The stars don't glow anymore.
They look like bruises now.
My journals are there.
Stacked. Fragile.
I open one and find no words, just long lines where sentences used to be.
As if the ink evaporated with my voice.
As if even my handwriting couldn't survive the weight of remembering.
In the corner of the room, the red anklet.
Always the red anklet.
It doesn't jingle anymore.
It just sits, curled like a sleeping question.
I don't pick it up.
I know what it did.
You don't think of rooms as living things.
But they are.
They inhale you.

They digest your laughter, your weeping, your silences.
They store your ghosts like wallpaper patterns.

I once told someone I wanted to be loved like a locked room.
He laughed. Said I was too dramatic.
But the truth was—I didn't want someone to open me.
I just wanted someone to knock.

The last room on this hallway—I haven't opened yet.
The knob is cold. The air outside it stings.
I think it holds the moment everything ended.

But I'm not brave enough to enter.

Instead, I sit in the hallway, listening to the hum of things that never stopped happening.
A door creaks. A cup falls in some old kitchen.
Footsteps—mine or hers, I can't tell.

I used to think memories fade.
But they don't.
They just change shape.

They become furniture in rooms you stop visiting.
Until one day, you walk by—and the chair has your name carved into it.
And you remember.

I remember.

14

CELLER

---♡---

"Grief is a thread you wear even after the wound stops bleeding."

I don't remember tying it.

The red thread around my ankle—it was just there.

One day, soft as breath. The next, tight as a warning.

I used to think it was tradition. Some holy thing.

Now I know it was a scar in disguise.

They say threads carry blessings.

But mine carries screams.

It whispers to me in moments when the world goes still—

when there are no clocks, no footsteps, no voices left to pretend I was never lonely.

In those moments, the thread tightens, and I remember.

Not all at once.

But in sharp, stinging stitches.

I remember the day I was pulled back from the river.

The water still in my lungs. My mouth refusing to speak.

And how someone—my mother, maybe—tied the thread tighter.

As if a knot could undo what the current almost welcomed.

No one asked why I walked into the water.

They just fed me sweets. Told me to sleep with the light on.
But they never untied the thread.
They thought if it stayed, so would I.
But grief isn't a person who runs.
It's a person who stays.
Even when your body doesn't.
I touch the thread sometimes.
It feels colder than it should.
Like metal spun into silk.
Like memory braided with mourning.
And it itches.
Not on the skin—
in the soul.
Like it knows I've outgrown it but can't let go.
You see, no one tells you how to mourn the girl you used to be.
They tell you how to bury people.
How to cry at funerals.
But what about when the funeral is internal?
When you are both mourner and corpse?
There are nights I try to untie it.
But it fights back.
It pulls tighter, like it's afraid of being forgotten.
Maybe it is.
Maybe this thread is all that's left of who I was.
Not the voice. Not the letters. Not even Zill.
Just a red line, circling me like a question I never answered.
If I ever find the beginning, maybe I'll find the end.
Maybe it leads somewhere.
Maybe it leads back to the day the silence began.
Or the day I mistook pain for prayer.

Or the hour my heart became a wound too polite to bleed.
I once read that in some cultures, red threads connect soulmates.
If that's true—
then grief is the one I was tied to.
And she's never letting go.

15
CRADLE

"Nothing lasts. Not even the things that pretend to."

Everything rots.

Even the things that are supposed to keep you alive.

Even love, even names, even prayers muttered under someone else's god.

I used to think salt was sacred—something to preserve, to purify.

Now I know it only slows the decay.

It never stops it.

I was thirteen when I first tasted salt that wasn't from the kitchen.

It came from my own face.

Tears I didn't know I was allowed to cry.

I remember licking my lips and thinking—so this is how sadness tastes.

After that, it was everywhere.

In the way my mother cooked too much food for too few people.

In the sweat on my neck during nights that refused to cool down.

In the blood from the time I fell, and no one noticed.

Even in my language.
Ballia has a word for sorrow that sounds like a sigh being
swallowed.

I think grief is made of salt.
That's why it stings the eyes.
That's why it never evaporates.
It just sits. Clings. Crystallizes.
They say wounds need salt to cleanse.
But what about the wounds that never wanted healing?
What about the ones you carry like jewelry,
because even pain is better than forgetting?
You want honesty?
Here it is:
There is no meaning.
Not in pain.
Not in survival.
Not even in death.
I didn't die so I could be remembered.
I didn't suffer so I could be made beautiful in someone's
poetry.
There is no soft lesson in this.
There's just a girl with a throat full of sand,
and a stomach that hasn't known warmth in years.
There's just a red anklet that mocks me with every ghost-
step.
There's just a long line of doors that lead to more grief, more
silence, more rot.
And salt.
Always salt.

I dream of oceans, not because they're beautiful,
but because they hold everything that was thrown away.
Sometimes I imagine myself sinking into one.
Letting the water fill every hollow in me,
until the salt finally does what it was meant to—
make me disappear.
But even then, I know the body floats before it sinks.
Even in death, we resist release.
Isn't that tragic?
That even the dead have to wait?
No gods came.
No light.
No peace.
Just salt.
And the awful taste of remembering that nothing—
not even me—was ever meant to last.

16

SCAB

"I broke so quietly, no one heard it happen."
There was no noise when it happened.
No cinematic crack.
No falling to the floor in pieces.
No blood.
Just me, one evening, sitting on the edge of a bed that didn't feel like mine, staring at my own hands like they belonged to someone I didn't trust.
I had stopped crying months before.
Not because the pain was gone—
but because I had finally run out of salt.
People expect collapse to be a performance.
But most of the time, it's a posture.
You sit a little differently.
Your eyes stop reaching for light.
You drink tea without tasting it.
You stop brushing your hair because no one's going to touch it anyway.
That's how glass breaks.
I don't remember when I stopped laughing.
Only that one day someone told me I was quieter than I

used to be,
and I wanted to say,

"Quieter isn't the word. I just disappeared."
But I didn't.
Because by then, I had already learned how to fold myself small enough to be overlooked.

I was made of glass.
And glass is not fragile because it's weak.
It's fragile because it remembers every pressure that ever touched it.
And even if it holds—

the strain is still there, spider-webbing beneath the surface, waiting for the moment someone looks away.

The thing about being made of glass is that you become obsessed with control.
You count your steps.
You lower your voice.
You cross your legs, smile softly, keep your hands visible.

You rehearse being harmless.

Because you know—one wrong move and everything will fall.
And worse, it won't even make a sound they'll care about.

My body still walks.
It eats, sometimes.
It even sleeps.

But it doesn't hold anymore.
It doesn't keep warmth.
It doesn't carry hope.

There's a kind of silence that lives in the bones.
A hush that settles where trust used to be.
I don't even miss the people who left anymore.
I just miss the version of me that still waited for them.
I've been gathering pieces for years now.
Tiny reflections of the girl I once was—
shards of joy, splinters of touch, slivers of belief that
someone might come back.
But I can't glue her back together.
I wouldn't even know where to start.
And even if I did, what's the point?
Repaired glass is never whole.
It's something else.
Something more fragile, not less.
They call it resilience.
I call it exhaustion.
When people ask how I'm doing now,
I tell them I'm fine.
But what I really mean is:
I've learned how to bleed without a mess.
And sometimes that's all survival is.
Not healing.
Not growing.
Just staying intact enough that no one notices the crack
across your chest.

17
KNELL

"Some girls learn to pray. Others learn to bite."
I wasn't born angry.
But grief has teeth, and I learned to grow mine early.
No one teaches little girls how to scream.
They teach us how to lower our voices, how to fold our rage into politeness, how to swallow the no before it reaches our lips.
They didn't know I was choking on everything I never said.
I used to think anger was something ugly.
Something loud, masculine, dangerous.
But now I know—it can be quiet.
Anger can wear a soft voice and a clean dress.
It can sit at the dinner table and smile through broken molars.
I remember the first time I clenched my fists so hard my nails left crescents in my palm.
I kept my hands hidden all day, ashamed that I'd tried to hold in the flood and failed.
But no one asked.
No one saw the blood.

Because I was good at being gentle.
I was taught to be gentle.
To be agreeable.
To be liked.
But I never learned how to say Stop.
Or Don't touch me.
Or I'm not okay.
So I grew teeth instead.
Not the kind you see when I smile.
The kind in my stomach,
my throat,
my spine.
I bit down on my grief until it forgot how to speak.
I chewed through the days pretending they tasted like something sweet.
But everything was ash.
Everything was bark.
Sometimes I dream of screaming.
Not at anyone.
Just into a room that can finally echo it back.
Just to hear the sound of my voice not asking for permission.
I've spent years apologizing for my existence.
For my anger.
For my sadness.
For not being the version of myself that people liked better—quieter, kinder, less.
But I'm not sorry anymore.

I'm angry that I had to grow teeth just to survive.
That I had to protect myself from people who said they loved me.

That I had to hide my fire to make others comfortable in the
dark.
    And now?
Now I know what I'm made of.
    I am not soft.
I am not sugar.
I am not salvageable.
    I am teeth.
And I have learned how to use them.

18

RELIQUARY

"After the fire, there is no light. Just smoke. Just silence. Just me."
Everything that mattered once has turned to smoke.
I walk through the ruins of my own memory now.
I touch what's left, and it turns to powder on my fingers.
There's no going back.
There's nothing left to go back to.
I burned it all.
Or maybe it burned without me even noticing.
That's the thing about slow pain—it doesn't scream.
It smolders.
Quietly.
Patiently.
Until one day, the walls are black, and you're still standing
in the center asking what went wrong.
The truth?
I used to be full of color.
I swear I did.
I loved like fire.
I spoke like dawn.
I laughed like I believed I would live forever.
And now?

Now I don't even look in mirrors.
There's nothing I want to see there.

When I speak, my voice sounds like it's coming from somewhere far away.
Like a ghost trying to remember the shape of a name.
I've stopped waiting for the phone to ring.
Stopped checking if they texted back.
Stopped writing drafts of conversations that will never happen.
People keep saying healing is coming.
But what if it already did?
What if this—this emptiness, this ache, this gray—is all that's left of it?
What if healing isn't light?
What if healing is just ash?
And maybe that's enough.
Maybe survival isn't about blooming again.
Maybe it's about sitting in the charred remains of yourself and saying:
I'm still here.
That's all I can do.
I sit with the ruins.
I name what was lost.
I breathe.
No hope.
No prayers.
Just breath.

Because sometimes, after everything has burned, the bravest thing you can do is not run.
You stay.
You gather the ash in your hands.

You whisper to it like it's sacred.
     And you let it fall.
One last time.

19
THRESHOLD

"There's a room in my mind where I never stopped being fifteen.
I visit her often. She never looks up.

    I keep going back there.

    To the room.

It changes shape sometimes, but it's always the same feeling.

A single chair.

A bed no one has slept in for years.

A window that refuses to open.

    The light in that room is always tired.

It's not sunlight.

It's the kind of light that stays behind when the world moves on.

The kind that doesn't touch anything.

Just lingers.

    She's always there—

the younger version of me.

The one before the breaking.

She sits on the floor with her back against the wall,

her knees pulled to her chest like she's trying to disappear inward.

She doesn't cry.
She just waits.
I used to think she was waiting for someone.
Now I know she's waiting for me.
Every time I visit, I try to speak.
But my voice doesn't work in this place.
Words get caught in my throat like they're afraid to be heard.
Sometimes I want to scream:
"You make it! We make it! You survive!"
But I don't.
Because it wouldn't be true.
She survives, yes.
But she never stops being afraid.
She grows older, learns how to smile on command, learns how to laugh in the right places.
She learns how to walk with her arms crossed tight across her chest like armor.
She learns how to leave rooms before they leave her.
But she never really escapes that one room.
Neither do I.
Some nights, I lie awake and feel her breathing beside me.
Not like a ghost.
More like a bruise.
A weight I carry with reverence and exhaustion.
I want to ask her what she remembers.
What moment did it all start to go dim?
Was it the silence after the shouting?
Was it the night she curled up under the desk and listened to her own heartbeat thudding like a knock?
Was it the first time someone said "I love you" and didn't mean it?

The room holds it all.
The first betrayal.
The first time she bled and told no one.
The first time she realized her body was a place people came
to forget themselves.
No one visits her but me.
And I don't even knock anymore.
I just open the door,
step in,
sit down across from her.
We don't speak.
We don't need to.
We just exist—two versions of the same girl—
one still breaking,
the other pretending she's healed.
This is the final chapter before the poem.
But not the end.
Because there's no end.
Only a room.
And the girl inside it.
Waiting.
Always waiting.

20

NOT EVEN THEN

❤

A poem in one breath, never meant to be read aloud.
There was once a girl who swallowed stars
thinking they were medicine—
and now the light inside her makes her sick.
She walks the edges of herself, barefoot,
feeling for cracks in the floor that is her name.
No one told her that being a body was a lifelong curse,
that even silence has a sound when it comes from within.
Even the mirror flinches.
She talks to the moon like it's a wound
and the moon listens like it's guilty.
Once, she prayed.
Then she begged.
Then she stopped.
God never answered.
But the ceiling always did.
At night, her hands search for softness—
but all she finds is skin stretched over memory.
All she finds is heat that doesn't belong to anyone.
Every room she's ever left still holds her outline.
And she's tired of being a ghost

in houses that no longer call her back.

    She remembers the red anklet.
The one she wore the day she stopped being a child.
It bit into her like truth.
And she let it.
    She tells herself stories now,
the kind with endings that don't hurt.
But they're lies.
They always were.
The prince never came.
The mother never stayed.
The sea never swallowed her gently.
    She writes letters she will never send
to people she wishes she never loved.
She signs none of them.
    In one version of her life, she lives.
In another, she never even makes it to sixteen.
But in this one—
this brutal, beautiful middle—
she walks alone.
    There is blood under her fingernails.
Not from fighting.
From digging.
    Digging for a pulse in a world
that keeps asking her to smile.

    She smiled once.
They said she looked better that way.
So she carved it in.
So she never forgot.

Somewhere, a girl is still knocking on a locked door.
Somewhere, a scream is still echoing through a ribcage.
Somewhere, someone is still calling her name.
But not here.
Not now.
And even if they did—
Not even then.

Author's Note

Author's Note

Some stories aren't written — they bleed out.
This was one of them.

Not Even Then is not just a book; it's a body left behind in the silence, a whisper through locked doors, a scream no one turned toward. I didn't write this to be brave. I wrote it because I wasn't. And maybe I still am not.

This book is for the ones who sat at the edge of their bed at 3 a.m., whispering "please, not me."
It's for the ones who spoke up and were called liars.
For the ones who were loud once, and then became quiet forever.
For the ones who wanted to grow old — but didn't get to.

Diya is not me.
But Diya is someone I know.
And Zill is the girl I still hope to protect — in others, and in myself.

If you've ever felt haunted by your own body, if you've ever questioned whether your pain was real just because no one else saw it — I want you to know: I did. I do. I will.

And if you ever find yourself standing at the edge, doubting your own voice, your own worth, your own truth —

I hope these pages remind you:
You were right to feel it.
You were always right to survive.
Even if no one believed you.
Even if you had to keep going without a name.

Even if the night swallowed everything.
    You mattered.
    You matter.
    Always.
Even now.
Not even then.
    — Niswita

About The Author

Niswita Singh was born and raised in a quiet village in Ballia, Uttar Pradesh — a place where stories lived in silence and hearts often spoke in whispers. She began writing when words were the only way she could hear herself. A literature student by heart and a poet by instinct, Niswita finds comfort in late-night diaries, delicate metaphors, and the way language softens even the sharpest truths.

Not Even Then is her first published work — born not from ambition, but from ache. She writes for the unheard, the unseen, the ones who were told to quiet down and smile anyway.

At 22, she still believes in the power of fragile things — a verse, a girl, a red anklet — and the way they survive in stories when they cannot in the world.

When not writing, she is either curled up with a book, scribbling in the margins of her thoughts, or losing herself in a sky full of metaphors.

You can connect with her on Instagram at @nishwitty or reach out via email: nishwitasingh@gmail.com